CINDERELLEPER

A Fairytale Satire

Ford Forkum

This book is dedicated to my family,
who I love like a stepfamily.

Actually, that was a lie. This book is really dedicated
to my friend Jamie DeBree, whose knowledge and
support helped to bring this book to life.

Once upon a time (here we go again), there was a young woman named Ella, whose early life could hardly be described as a fairytale, except in the literal sense, of course. When she was just a little girl, her mother passed away. Her father eventually remarried, but the woman he poorly chose as his new wife didn't like Ella, and neither did the woman's two daughters from a previous marriage.

In the early days of the new family arrangement, Ella tried desperately to please her stepmother and to get along well with her stepsisters. But her efforts were only met with rejection and meanness. It seemed the more she tried to please them, the worse they treated her. This troubled her greatly, but she was too young and emotionally vulnerable to understand the situation.

In one disturbing incident, as Ella was sweeping the kitchen, her stepmother expressed disapproval of her sweeping technique by grabbing the broom and snapping it in half over Ella's head. (Fortunately, it was a flimsy broomstick, but having it broken over her head still kind of hurt.)

In that moment, Ella began to suspect that the source of her difficulty in establishing harmonious relations might have something to do with her stepmother being a psychotic bitch.

The situation deteriorated into an absolute nightmare, and despite Ella's desperation, she failed to convince her father of how badly her stepfamily was treating her. The stepmother and her daughters were very manipulative and somehow able to minimize or explain away anything Ella complained about. And Ella's father was quite easy to deceive because although he was a kind man and loving father, he was also, unfortunately, an idiot.

One night, however, after the family had sat down to the dinner that Ella prepared, her stepmother took a bite of the main course and spat it out on her plate. "This roast isn't thoroughly cooked!" she shouted. "Are you trying to poison us?"

"No, ma'am," Ella replied. "In fact, I'm quite certain the roast has been sufficiently—"

"How dare you talk back to me!" her stepmother roared. "I'll kill you! I'll kill you, and then put *you* in the oven, and then we'll all have *you* for dinner!" She wiped her face with a napkin and continued: "That will teach you to properly cook a damn roast! No, on second thought, just get in the oven and we'll cook your ass alive!"

Everyone at the table fell silent. The stepsisters exchanged worried glances, to which the stepmother responded, "What's the matter with you two? You look like you've seen a banshee or something!"

The elder stepsister cleared her throat and pointed in the father's general direction. The father, who was sitting right next to the stepmother, was staring at her with bulging eyes and a gaping jaw. When the stepmother turned to look at him, she realized how badly she screwed up. She laughed nervously and said, "I was simply joking! Of course I'd never intentionally kill sweet, young Ella for undercooking my dinner! How could you possibly think I was serious?"

Ella stood up and rushed to her father's side, and took his hand. "Father, we need to speak in private right now!" They went upstairs to Ella's bedroom, where she thoroughly explained and finally made the situation clear to him.

He hugged his dear daughter, apologized for being a negligent ignoramus, and angrily left the bedroom to confront his wife. He gently closed the bedroom door behind him and walked across the wooden floor toward the stairs. Just as he was about to turn and descend the staircase, he slipped on a banana peel one of the stepsisters had carelessly dropped on the floor, tumbled noisily and clumsily down the stairs, and died.

***

They say, "life sucks, then you die," but in Ella's case it was, "Life is good, then your mother dies, your father remarries an evil psychopath with two horrible daughters, and then your father dies, and you continue to live."

One would think that any mother who allegedly cared for her own children would take pity on a girl who lost both her parents before coming of age. One might also think that two girls who had "mysteriously" lost their own father would sympathize with their stepsister's loss.

Unfortunately, that's not how it worked out, and things only got worse. With Ella's father out of the picture, her stepfamily had free reign to treat her however they damn well pleased, and were delighted to have a fully qualified slave around the house. Ella's broken spirit assured them she would be docile and complicit.

In addition to running her ragged, they took ownership of all her possessions and forced her to sleep in the unfinished basement on a straw mat by the fireplace. She would often wake up in the mornings spotted with ashes, which her stepsisters found amusing.

Since they didn't allow her to bathe or wash her one article of clothing very often, the ashes would tend to accumulate.

On one occasion, she came up from the basement to find her stepsisters waiting for her.

"Look at Ella!" the older one said, pointing. "There she is again, all covered with cinders!"

"Hey," said the younger. "We should call her 'Cinder Ella!'"

"Hah, ha, yeah! What do you think of that, 'Cinderella?'"

Cinderella said nothing, not having the will to stand up for herself. Apparently, her new nickname stuck quickly. As contrived and uncreative as it was, it had an oddly iconic ring to it. Go figure.

***

Meanwhile, across town at the royal palace, the queen was having a talk with her only son, the prince. The queen sat rigidly on her throne as the prince, a strikingly handsome, tall, and broad-shouldered young man with abs to die for, listened reluctantly.

"As you know, son," she said. "We're having yet another grand ball for you in three days, and we're inviting every woman of marrying age in the land. And this time, the king and I demand of you to finally choose a wife."

The prince, looking down, sniveled and scratched at his nostril.

The queen frowned. "Are you listening to me?" she asked.

The prince, his eyes on the floor and his hands in his coat pockets, gently kicked at the base of the throne. "Yeah, ma, I heard you! But I wish you'd let me put off getting married a little while longer. I don't feel like I'm ready to give up orgies."

The queen sighed. "You can still have orgies, but, for the sake of the kingdom, you must marry and bear children."

"Well, why can't I just marry Cousin Edwina?"

"Because, as I've told you, our family line desperately needs new genetic material. Collectively, we're beginning to look like a sideshow attraction that has a small group of spectators."

"But why do I have to be the one to marry a stranger?"

"Because you're one of the few spectators, and the highest-ranking one among them. We're all depending on you, son. And you'd better take this seriously! If you don't choose a mate this time, you'll get no dessert for a week!"

The prince sneered as he continued staring at the floor. "All right, fine, I'll do it, ma! Jeez, you don't hafta threaten me!"

***

Getting back to Cinderella, the squalid conditions she was forced to live in and the rancid food her stepmother fed her caused her to fall ill. Begrudgingly, the stepmother brought her to see a doctor. As the doctor examined her, her stepmother waited outside in the family coach.

After performing several tests, and confirming his findings, the doctor entered the room where Cinderella was waiting. "I have good news and bad news." He said. "The good news is, your symptoms are the result of a simple infection, and should clear up with some medicine." He handed her a vial of some green elixir.

"What's the bad news?"

"You have terminal leprosy."

"Leprosy?" Cinderella cried. "Oh my God! Isn't that the disease where people's body parts just fall off?"

"That almost never happens," the doctor replied.

"Oh, good," Cinderella sighed.

"However, in your case, it most likely will," said the doctor.

"Oh, God!" Cinderella cried.

"Yes. Unfortunately, you have that ultra-rare, almost mythical form of the disease, where, if I were to pull on your nose and say, 'I got your nose,' it would be ironic because I literally *would* 'get your nose.' And I if I tried to put it back on, it wouldn't stay."

Cinderella buried her face in her hands and wept. The doctor gently placed his hand on her back. "Now, child, it's not the end of the world. You're in the early stages and won't experience any symptoms for...probably several days. And, when your body parts start falling off, you won't feel a thing. It will be like shedding skin, except you'll also shed bone or cartilage and so forth."

Cinderella kept crying.

The doctor took a few steps forward to wipe some dust off a chart on the wall. "And it all happens cleanly," he continued. "New skin forms in the area of detachment, so there's no bleeding involved, and no possibility for infection. It's like amputation without the need for anesthesia or stitches, or even a surgeon."

Cinderella kept crying.

"The only thing you'll need to be careful of is that it tends to happen out of the blue. You know, one minute you're fine, and then all of a sudden you go numb somewhere and, whoops, there goes your middle finger. It can be embarrassing, but at least the part that falls off won't get all gross and nasty for a while. It can even make an interesting conversation piece if you play it off right."

Having grown tired of the doctor's astounding failure to comfort her, Cinderella gave up crying. She lifted her head and stared at him in puffy-eyed resignation.

The doctor removed his glasses to fog up the lenses with his breath and wipe them off. "It's actually a fascinating illness," he said. "Medical science has very little knowledge of how it all works. It's not contagious and we don't know what causes it. We only know how to diagnose it. Your case would be a great opportunity for research and experimentation to find a cure. It's just a shame I can't take that opportunity."

"Why not?"

"Because there's no money in it. I'm running a business here, not a charity. Which reminds me: hold on for a minute while I prepare your bill."

Cinderella trudged out of the office and toward the family carriage where her stepmother was waiting to prod her for the diagnosis. "Well, what's wrong with you?"

"I—"

"Besides everything. In particular, I mean. What did the

doctor say you've got? Indigestion? Post-nasal drip?"

"I don't want to talk about it," she replied.

"Come on, Ella! If you can't tell your own stepmother, who can you tell?"

"No one. My condition is no one's business but my own."

"Now, Ella, I know I'm often hard on you, and maybe even a bit cruel and sadistic sometimes, and, truth be told, some days the only thing capable of bringing a smile to my face is making you suffer, but deep down you must know I really care about you."

"I don't believe you."

"Ella, if I didn't care, I wouldn't have taken you to see the doctor! Please, you must tell me. I'm very worried."

Cinderella huffed and brought her fingertips to her forehead. "All right, fine. I have leprosy. But don't worry! The doctor says it isn't contagious."

The stepmother pursed her lips tightly and slowly bent over with a sputtering snicker that sounded like "Pthzz thzz thzz thzz thzz thzz!" Inhaling and straightening back up, she threw head back and shouted, "Ha! Leprosy! Oh, you wretched thing! Cinderella, the leper!"

As her stepmother howled with laughter and slapped herself on the knees, Cinderella frowned and crossed her arms. "Oh, my," she said sarcastically. "I would never expect this kind of reaction out of you. How could you possibly find this funny? Oh, wait, I know. It's because you're a total cu—"

"I can't wait to tell my daughters!" the stepmother interrupted. "We're going to have to start calling you…Cinderelleper! Ha, ha, ha! What do you think of that, 'Cinderelleper?'"

Cinderelleper said nothing and continued to stare vacantly at the road ahead. Apparently, the new nickname stuck as quickly as her former one.

**

Returning home, the stepmother burst through the door. "Oh, girls!" she called with a melodic inflection. "Guess who has leprosy!"

The girls trotted down the stairs to greet their mother and get the scoop. "Did you say leprosy?" one of them asked.

"Yes! Can you believe it? And I've decided that, from now on, we're going to call her Cinderelleper."

The sisters exchanged glances and then exploded with laughter. Their mother joined them.

Cinderelleper trudged off to her straw mat in the basement. The mental cruelty of her stepfamily was so warped that she couldn't seriously suffer any hurt feelings by this point. With her future compromised by a terminal disease, she was far less concerned about placating them as well. She played up her sad trudge in the hopes that they would be satisfied enough to leave her alone for a while.

"Mother," the younger stepsister said as she wiped a tear from her eye. "When is she going to die?"

The stepmother suddenly looked serious. "I don't know," she replied, "but I'd better get looking for another husband with a kid to replace her. I'll be damned if we're going back to doing our own housework."

Just then the doorbell rang. The stepmother turned around and opened the door to see a man in ceremonial attire: a messenger from the royal palace.

"Well, hello, my good man," she said in a slow, affectedly pleasant voice. "What brings you to my doorstep on this lovely afternoon?"

"Tidings from the king and queen," the man replied. "You and the three young ladies of this residence are cordially invited to attend the grand ball in honor of the prince two days hence."

The stepmother's eyes widened and she grinned. "Oh? He's having another ball?"

"Yes, milady. Yet another one."

"Goodness! I know it's not my place to say anything about it, but the prince certainly has a lot of balls!"

The messenger blinked nonchalantly. "Indeed," he replied, "while making my rounds, I've heard that comment a number of times today. An overwhelming number of times, in fact. If I hear it again, I may—"

"So, is he finally going to select a bride, or is he getting everyone's hopes up for nothing again?"

"Rest assured, this time the king and queen mean business. They've threatened to restrict his dessert privileges for an entire week."

"Oh, that is good news. Please tell the royal family we'll be delighted to attend. My daughters are very fond of the prince, you know."

The messenger rolled his eyes. "Yes, milady, it seems the prince has many ambitious admirers."

"Ah, but none as eager to please or as gifted with, ahem, certain talents as my daughters." She opened the door wider to reveal the stepsisters standing near the bottom of the stairs, grinning from ear to ear, winking at the messenger, waving flirtatiously, blowing kisses, and generally being as embarrassingly unsubtle as humanly possible.

The messenger shuddered and looked over his shoulder. "Milady, I regret I must keep to a tight schedule and be on my way."

"Well, if you must…but please give my regards to the king and queen."

"Good day."

The stepmother slowly shut the door. "Yes!" she shouted. "All right girls, this is your final opportunity to hit the marriage jackpot!"

"The prince is going to choose me!" the older stepsister said.

"No, me!" the younger stepsister argued.

Smiling, the stepmother shrugged her shoulders and turned up her palms. "What freaking difference does it make? As long as one of you bags him, we'll all be living the sweet life!"

***

In the days leading up to the ball, Cinderelleper was mostly left alone by the other women of the house. They were too preoccupied with the ball to bother her despite their curiosity as to which part of her was going to fall off first.

But just before they left on the night of the ball, they made sure to parade themselves before her in their glorious ballroom attire. "Well, Cinderelleper," the stepmother said. "We're off to spend the evening at the palace for the royal ball in honor of his majesty, the prince."

Cinderelleper remained motionless on her straw mat on the

floor. "Have fun," she replied, without a hint of enthusiasm. "I'll just stay here and rot."

"Well, after tonight, you can have the house to yourself, because your stepsisters and I are moving into the palace! Come on, girls! Let's bag ourselves a horny prince!" They went up the basement stairs and out the front door.

The house was dark, save for the fireplace, and all was quiet. Cinderelleper sat up on her straw mat and looked up through the window at the starry night sky. Staring deep into space, she thought about her mother. "Soon, mother," she whispered. "Soon we'll be together again. If you're with father, please punch him in the face for me. I miss you."

As she stared, a cloud blocking the moon drifted slowly away, and the full moon shone down a beam of light so intense it made her squint and turn away. She rubbed her eyes for a few seconds and opened them to see a kindly old woman standing in front of her. "Hello, Ella," the old woman said soothingly.

Cinderelleper rubbed her eyes again, but the old woman was either no hallucination or a very persistent one. She backed away until her back hit the wall. "Who are you?" she asked. "How did you get here?"

"I'm your fairy godmother," the old woman replied. "And I've come from Fairy Godmotherland to help you save the kingdom!"

"Me? Save the kingdom?" Cinderelleper asked. "But I'm on death's doorstep!"

"Ah, but there's still time for you to fulfill a great destiny!"

"What destiny?"

"You see, dear, tonight the prince will choose a woman

outside the royal family to be the princess. Your stepmother will stop at nothing to gain access to the royal family's power. And if she succeeds in marrying off either of your stepsisters to the prince, the entire kingdom will fall to ruin!"

"Oh, my! What kind of twisted scheme is my stepmother plotting?"

"She's not plotting anything. But can you *imagine* the keys to the castle in the hands of that mad harpy? Total ruin would be inevitable!"

Cinderelleper gasped.

"Your mission is clear. You must win the prince's heart to ensure that your stepsisters fail, despite the fact they probably would without your involvement."

"But how am I going to do that? I'm dirty, dressed in rags, and I don't even have a ride to the palace! Also, I'm a leper!"

"I'll show you how. Come outside with me!"

The fairy godmother flew up the basement stairs. Cinderelleper followed her out the door and into the yard, where a pumpkin and several mice awaited. The fairy rolled up her sleeves and waved her magic wand. Little particles of white, sparkly light emanated from the wand, and from an invisible harp, a rapid succession of ascending notes could be heard. "Now for the magic incantation!" she bellowed. "Bonkerty, Bopperty, Boob!"

The pumpkin transformed into a coach, several of the mice into horses, and one of the mice into a human being, ostensibly, to drive the coach.

The fairy turned to Cinderelleper. "…And since you can't go to the grand ball looking like a crackwhore…"

With another wave of her wand, she adorned her with the classiest gown and accessories magic could produce, right down to a pair of dazzling, but insensible slippers made of glass.

"Oh this is so beautiful and wonderful!" said Cinderelleper. "Everything is perfect! Except…what's up with the coach?"

"What do you mean, dear?"

"I'm certainly not complaining, but you're powerful enough to turn mice into fully sentient human beings, right?"

"Well, he's not exactly sentient, dearie. I mean, he can obey simple commands and make minimal conversation, but if you ask him what the meaning of life is, he'll probably tell you it's to find cheese and procreate."

"That's not my point, Godma. I'm talking about the coach. You can make mice into people and yet you can't make a coach out of a pumpkin that doesn't look like anything but a giant, hollowed-out, horse-drawn pumpkin on wheels?"

The fairy winked. "Young Ella, I know you don't get around much, but these days, the pumpkin look is all the rage in designer coaches!"

"Well, that's…odd, but I guess it's better than those foreign carriages that have the horses in back, pushing with their heads."

"Yes, those are ridiculous. But enough talk; time is short! Just keep in mind that the spell will wear off by midnight. The coach will turn back into a pumpkin, the horses and driver will turn back into mice, and you'll go back to looking like Courtney Love. Make sure you're out of the palace and on the road well before then!"

"Okay, Godma, but can I ask you a favor?"

"Certainly, my dear."

"Do you think, maybe, you could conjure up a spell and, you know, cure my leprosy?"

"I'm sorry, dear, but the answer is no. I'm a fairy, not a miracle worker."

"Just thought I'd ask."

"But the prince doesn't need to know you're a leper. In fact, it might be a good idea not to bring it up. It could put a damper on the attraction."

Cinderelleper took a few steps toward the coach, stopped, and looked back at the fairy. "I still don't get this. What's the point of getting the prince to marry me if I'm just going to die on him before I can bear him any children?"

"Sweetie, you're an intelligent, kind, and beautiful young lady. You don't have to win the prince's heart. All you have to do is contrast with your stepsisters to remind the prince to choose his bride wisely. A little trash-talking wouldn't hurt either; just be subtle about it and don't come off like a backstabber. Nobody likes a backstabber."

"I suppose I've got to do what I can to save the kingdom."

The godmother winked. "Not to mention, turnabout is fair play."

Cinderelleper grinned slyly, waved good-bye and strutted toward the coach. "Screw the kingdom," she thought to herself. "This is personal."

The coach driver got down from his seat to open the door for her. "Hi, Lady!" he said childishly. "I am driver. I like cheese. Do you like cheese?"

"Yes, I like cheese, but probably not as much as you do. Do you know the way to the palace?"

"Yes, I know way to palace. Palace and home. And places where there is cheese."

"Good. Then let's go."

"Yes, Lady!" he responded, climbed back up into his seat, and grabbed the reigns. "Okay, horsies, giddyup!" And the coach was on its way, bouncing and banging over the rugged terrain.

Cinderelleper rested her head in her hands, silently sulking as her head jostled around.

After a thoroughly uncomfortable ride, she arrived at the steps to the palace entrance.

***

Inside the ballroom, the prince stood in the center of the dance floor and called the room to attention.

"All right, everyone, shut up and listen!" he shouted. "The guards just closed the ballroom door, so anyone who shows up now ain't getting in! If you were expecting to meet someone here and you haven't already, you're outta luck. Anyway, to make this easy, I'm gonna start the night by dancing with those of you I haven't met before or don't remember. So, if you haven't been here before, stand in line by the punchbowl. The rest of you whores will have to wait your turn."

He turned around to face the back of the room, where the orchestra was waiting for his cue to begin playing. He stared contemptuously for a few seconds and shouted, "Well, what are you waiting for? Start playin', ya bunch of pansies!"

The conductor's coat tails flared as he spun around and motioned for the orchestra to begin. The strains of a lively waltz filled the air and many couples began walking toward the dance floor.

The prince's face turned red as he grit his teeth and waved his arms at the orchestra. The music stopped unevenly and the prince shouted again. "What the hell are you doing?" he bellowed. "That tune sucks!"

"Apologies, your highness!" the conductor shouted back. "Would you prefer that we avoid playing waltz music?"

"Yeah, no!" the prince replied. "I don't know who that guy Walt is, but his tunes are friggin' gay! Don't play his stuff!"

"Yes, your highness."

The orchestra began again and the prince finally walked over to the line of hopeful young women. He made his way toward the head of the line, and commented loudly with a pointed finger as he walked past each woman: "Ugly, ugly, wicked ugly, fat, too tall, ugly." He stopped at Cinderelleper. "All right, let's go." He took her by the hand and marched to the center of the dance floor, shoving people aside along the way.

As they began dancing, he struck up a conversation. "So, babe," he said. "How do you like my ball?"

Cinderelleper nervously cleared her throat. "It's impressive, your highness," she remarked. "I've never seen so many people."

"Yeah," the prince said. "No one in the land can turn down an invitation to my balls. You see the duke over there?"

Cinderelleper turned her head and gazed across the room. "Is he the one trying to discretely pull the wedgie out of his butt?"

"Yeah, that's him. He's known for packing some seriously huge balls. And then there's the countess, that drunken slag yelling at the curtains, she has some big-ass balls herself."

Cinderelleper blinked in mild confusion. "Is it customary for the women of our land to have balls?"

"Yeah, but it's not normal. Anyway, I've got 'em both licked." He continued with a smug grin. "Neither one of them can hold a candle to my balls, 'cause I've got the biggest balls of them all."

Somewhere in the distance, a cow mooed in agony from having been milked dry.

Back in the ballroom, the song came to a close, and the prince dismissed her. "All right, time for me to check out some of these other bimbos," he said. "But stick around. I've got a feeling you 'n' me are gonna dance again." The prince headed back toward the line at the punchbowl, and Cinderelleper walked away in the opposite direction. It wasn't long before someone else asked her to dance.

She found herself being asked to dance nearly every time a new piece of music began. As the night wore on, she found herself, for the first time since she could remember, having fun. Eventually, she grew tired and found a chair to rest in.

She closed her eyes and listened to the orchestral music and the pleasant murmur around her. After relaxing to several of the orchestra's pieces, she decided to head over to the banquet table to get something delicious to eat. But as soon as she opened her eyes and leaned forward to stand up, she was startled to notice her stepmother advancing directly toward her, with the stepsisters in tow.

"Oh, God, they've spotted me," she said to herself. She looked to her left and then to her right, but there was no point in trying to run away; they'd only confront her later. She stood up straight and looked her stepmother in the eye as they came within speaking range. Deciding to take the initiative, she began to address her stepmother. "Hello, Mo—"

"Look, kid," she interrupted. "I don't know who you are or

where you come from, but my daughters haven't had a turn with the prince tonight!"

Cinderelleper gawked at her. "You…don't know who I am?" she asked.

"No, and I don't care! The point is, you and all the other new girls had better stay away from the prince, or else!"

"Yeah!" the stepsisters shouted in agreement.

Cinderelleper rapidly shook her head. "Wait," she said. "You three seriously have no idea who I am?"

"I told you, you hussy," the stepmother said, "I don't care!"

A sly smirk crossed Cinderelleper's face, and she took a step forward and jabbed a pointed finger at her stepmother's sternum. "Well, you'd better care!" she shouted. "I'm a duchess, you hag, and I could have your head on a silver platter!"

Humbled, the stepmother apologized and dismissed herself, leaving Cinderelleper smiling uncontrollably.

After many more dances and pleasant conversations, Cinderelleper glanced at the clock. It was 11:40, and the prince had not danced with either of her stepsisters the entire time. She felt certain the kingdom would be safe, and decided it was time to get going.

Just then, the orchestra stopped playing, and the prince, now inebriated, addressed the ballroom once more. "Listen up, p-people," he slurred. "I've been looking around for the first chick I danced with tonight. I wanna dance again, so if you're still here, bring your sweet booty over here on the double."

Not wanting to be seen leaving after the prince had summoned her, Cinderelleper hesitantly sauntered toward him for a final dance. The prince acknowledged her approaching with a crooked smile. "There she is!" he said boisterously. Then, turning toward the orchestra, he waved his arm and shouted, "Start playin', fruitcakes!"

The music started up again, and the two engaged in an awkward tripping of the light fantastic as the prince drunkenly stumbled about. Cinderelleper tried not to stare apprehensively into the prince's eyes as they continued dancing, but she couldn't wait for the song to end. The prince, however, was just getting started.

"So, anyway, babe," he said, "I was thinking you're probably gonna be the one." He turned his face away and belched loudly. Turning back, he said, "Ain't that great? You'll never have to work or think for yourself, 'cause I'll make all the decisions. Just do as I say and you'll never have to worry about a thing!"

She didn't reply, and began to reconsider her role in saving the kingdom. With her leprosy, who knew how much time she had to live, anyway? Besides, foiling her stepmother's agenda might only be temporary. She decided that whatever time she had left, she wasn't going to debase herself by marrying a jackass like the prince. There was more dignity in wasting away alone on a straw mat, and, all things considered, the kingdom falling into ruin was probably for the best.

When the music stopped, she coldly thanked the prince and excused herself.

"Hey, hold on a minute!" the prince protested. "I think you're the one I want to marry! Yeah! You're the one!"

But, your highness," she said, feigning respect, "we've only danced for two songs. We hardly know each other! How could you possibly be sure you want to marry me?"

"Because you're the hottest chick in the whole place! You're a dead ringer for my cousin Edwina!"

Cinderelleper tried not to faint. "Well…" she said, blinking and touching her face with a gloved hand. "You sure know how to charm a girl, Prince."

The prince put his fists on his hips. "Heh, don't I? I'm a prince, I'm a stud, and I'm mostly straight! What more could you want?"

"My dignity intact."

"Huh?"

Good night, your highness."

"No, wait!"

As she began to walk away, the Prince followed her. She walked faster. He stumbled faster behind her. As she rushed past a clock, she noticed it was almost midnight, and it dawned on her that if she didn't get to the coach in time, she might not be able to escape.

She ran as fast as she could out of the ballroom, out the palace doors and down the stairs toward the coach, with the prince doggedly pursuing her. "Hey! Get back here, bitch!"

As she neared the bottom of the staircase, she felt a tingling sensation in her ankle that quickly worsened to a numbing throughout her foot. One clumsy step down the last few stairs caused one of her glass slippers to come off, with her foot still inside it, as she fell to the ground.

Panicked, she got up and began hopping toward her horse-drawn pumpkin on wheels. She heard the doors at the top of the steps slamming open against the palace walls behind her. With a series of hops and a final leap through the window of the coach, she ordered the driver to speed away as quickly as possible.

The driver was slow to react, as if coming out of a dormant state. He turned around and noticed Cinderelleper lying face down on the coach floor with her legs hanging out the window.

"Hi, Lady!" he said, grinning. "How was ball?"

Cinderelleper turned her head to glare at him. "I had a blast!" she screamed, with her hair in her face. "Now, move it, mouse-brain!"

The driver fearfully snapped the reigns and the horses took off. As they sped through the night wind, and made their escape from the palace grounds, Cinderelleper lifted herself up by her arms and looked out the rear window. There was no sign of the prince. She grunted as she hauled herself into a seated position in the cart, leaning back against the seat with an intense sigh.

Feeling her movements inside the coach, the driver turned and looked behind him through the front window and turned back around with a frown. "Lady is mean to driver," he said aloud. "Lady thinks she is better than driver because she goes to balls and driver only drives. Lady has bad manners. Bad lady."

With concerted effort, Cinderelleper budged herself to the front edge of the seat. "You know what, driver?" she said. "I may be a one-footed leper slave, but I'll be damned if I take any crap from you. Because when this ride is over, you'll go right back to being nothing but a mouse: a dirty little buck-toothed ball of squeaking fur. So shut your mouth and drive me home so I can get back to dying on a straw mat in the basem—"

Her rant was interrupted by a chime from a nearby clock tower. She suddenly realized that if the coach turned back into a pumpkin at the speed they were traveling, she would be killed, or at least badly wounded, as she hit the ground. A second chime rang and she swallowed the lump in her throat.

"Driver!" she shouted. "Please stop the coach immediately!"

"Sorry," the driver replied. "Driver can't understand what Lady says. Driver is only a buck-toothed mouse."

"I didn't mean that! I'm sorry!" A fifth chime rang. "Please, I beg you, stop!'"

A sixth chime rang.

"You beg driver, Lady?"

"Yes! My life is entirely in your hands! You're now the most important person in the world to me!"

The ninth chime rang, and the driver reluctantly pulled the reigns. "Whoa, horsies," he said, and the horses began to slow down.

By the twelfth chime, the horses had come to a complete halt and instantly turned back into mice as the coach turned back into a pumpkin. Cinderelleper and the driver mouse fell to the ground, but because the coach had changed back with Cinderelleper inside it, it shrank to its original size around her waist, and cushioned her fall. In the process, it splattered as she landed on her butt.

The mice scurried about, all except the driver mouse, who sat up on his hind legs with his nose twitching, and seemed to look directly into Cinderelleper's eyes.

She stared back at the mouse. Feeling a strange sense of peace in the cool, quiet moonlight, she shrugged her shoulders and said, "So, you're a mouse. But I've no right to speak to you with anything but respect. I doubt you can understand this, but thank you for saving my life." She squirmed about in the pumpkin mess, and looked at her soiled clothes and footless leg. "…what's left of it, anyway."

Somehow, the mouse seemed to understand her words. He squeaked and moved closer to her.

Instinctively, Cinderelleper brought her hand to ground level with her palm facing up. "Well, Driver," she said, "you're welcome to stay with me on my straw mat by the fireplace. Maybe we can have some cheese together." The mouse sat motionless, contented in her gentle grip. "But, for the love of God, if you should happen to start singing, I may have to kill you." She slowly raised herself to a standing position, and with a grunt and a leap forward, began the four-and-a-half mile hop home.

Throughout her journey, she would periodically call out for help from her fairy godmother, but gave up after a few hours.

***

Late the next morning, she was awoken from her straw mat slumber by a knock at the front door. Her stepmother answered the door, excited to see the royal messenger again.

"Good day, milady," he said politely.

A manic smile lit up the stepmother's face. "I assume you have some good news for us, messenger?" she said, with clasped hands and batting eyelashes.

The messenger tried not to appear pained. "I have…news," he said. "The prince is looking for a particular woman he's chosen to be his bride."

"Who?" the stepmother asked. "Who is it?"

The messenger sighed. "He doesn't know, milady."

The stepmother frowned. "Let me get this straight," she said.

"You're telling me the prince has chosen a woman to be his bride, but he doesn't know who she is?"

"That is correct, milady."

"That doesn't even make sense! How could the prince possibly claim to have chosen someone to marry and yet not know who he's chosen?"

"You see, milady, he was very drunk last night, and can't remember who he chose. However, he does have a clue as to her identity."

"And what might that clue be?"

The messenger cleared his throat and tried not to feel like an idiot as he answered. "A foot."

"Excuse me, a foot?"

"Yes, milady. Now, did one of the young ladies of this house happen to lose a foot last night?"

"Is this a joke?"

"Most assuredly not, milady. Now, I need to know if any of the young ladies came home last night with one less foot than they left with."

The stepmother stared for a moment, and then, her eyes looked up in thought. "I...I'm not sure," she said. "I haven't seen any of them since last night. And I don't think they're around at the moment. Could you come back later?"

"Yes, milady. Upon conferring with the others in our search team, the prince and I will be returning later to all residences still in question. Good day."

The stepmother gently shut the door and watched from the window, waiting for the messenger to reach the next house. She called up the stairs. "Girls? Girls, are you here? I want to talk to you."

The stepsisters came down the stairs, and neither one was limping. The stepmother sighed and said, "Girls, it's over. The prince has decided whom he's going to marry, and it's apparently not one of you."

"But how do you know, mother?" asked the younger stepsister.

"Because whoever it is got into some kind of trouble last night at the ball, and her foot got severed. So the prince is going to be looking for some sorry wench with a stumpy leg. When he gets here and sees you two, he's going to be just as disappointed as I am."

The stepsisters were silent, each appearing lost in thought. After a few seconds, the younger one said. "Let him come. If the prince is going to reject me, I want him to tell me to my face."

"That's how I feel, too," the older one responded. "Anyway, I've got to get going. I have to get…something done."

"Yes," said the younger sister, eyeing the older one suspiciously. "I've got to be going, too."

Overhearing the conversation from the basement, Cinderelleper decided to stay put and remain silent. The only way out of the basement was up the stairs and through the house, and she didn't want to risk being discovered while trying to hop her way out.

***

Several hours later, the older stepsister returned home. She hadn't even made it through the front door when the stepmother accosted her. "Where have you been?" she asked.

The stepsister hobbled her way in with a cane. "I had a 'procedure,'" she said with a cunning grin.

"What kind of procedure?"

The stepsister lifted her dress to reveal a bandaged leg. "I had my foot amputated so I could fool the prince!"

The stepmother stared at her in shock. But after a few moments the shock faded away and she smiled. "My dear, precious daughter," she said. "I'm so proud of you!"

"Thank you, Mother. It was tough finding someone who could get it done on such short notice and not kill me in the process, and I'm high as a kite right now, so I don't feel a thing—"

"Yes, that's fine, dear, I don't need to know the details. Now, let's get you dolled up for the prince!"

After another hour or so had passed, the younger stepsister returned home, bursting into the doorway. "The prince is coming! The prince is coming!" she shouted. "His coach just turned down our street and is heading this way!"

Indeed the prince was on his way, along with the royal messenger, and, wearied from the search, neither one of them was having a particularly good afternoon.

They stopped in front of Cinderelleper's house. "This freakin' blows," said the hungover prince as he spilled out of the carriage. "Why do I gotta search the entire kingdom looking for some bitch who lost her foot when whoever it was could have just come to the palace?"

The messenger, beginning to feel that his entire life was nothing more than an endurance test against human stupidity, chose his response cautiously. "Your highness," he said. "You could have decided to do it that way from the start."

As they strolled up the walkway to Cinderelleper's house, the prince glared at the messenger. "Then why didn't I?" he shouted, accusingly.

Behind closed lips, the messenger grit his teeth. The words *because you're a contemptuous idiot slob who, by a mere accident of birth, was granted more power than you're capable of handling, and whose only rightful status in the kingdom is that of Village Idiot!* formed in his mind, but only materialized as an agonizing twinge in his shoulders.

Begrudgingly, the messenger knocked on the door, dreading the moment he would have to confront Cinderelleper's stepmother yet again.

"Please," he thought to himself. "Let them not be home."

Much to the his consternation, the stepmother answered the door, batting her eyelashes and putting on her usual nauseating display of sycophant fawning.

Repressing a longing to die on the spot, the messenger stated, "Milady, as you know, the prince and I are here to see if the aforementioned missing foot, which I am carrying in this satchel, belongs to one of the young ladies in this household. Since most of the women I spoke to earlier reported sustained bipedal functionality, and you weren't sure about your daughters, we've—"

"Shut the hell up, lackey," said the prince, barging in past the stepmother. "Let's just get this over with."

The stepmother responded cheerfully. "As it turns out, you've come to the right place!"

The messenger and prince entered the main living area, with the stepmother trotting behind, to find the older stepsibling seated eagerly on the living room sofa.

"Greetings, young lady," said the messenger. "As you know, we are here to return a glass slipper, along with a dismembered foot, to its rightful owner, and, in the process, find out whom the prince chose, in a state of near blacked-out inebriation, to be his life partner and princess of the royal—."

"Damn it, lackey, will you shut the hell up already?" the prince hollered. "They know why we're here!" The messenger meekly closed his lips, and the prince forcefully grabbed the satchel out of his hand.

The older stepsister cleared her throat and straightened her knee. From her seated position, the fabric of her gown fell away to reveal a footless, bandaged leg. "As you can see, Prince," she proclaimed, "it is I who am the one you're looking for."

The prince looked the stepsister over. "Really?" he asked aloud. "You're the one I chose?"

The stepsister meekly nodded with a grin.

The prince put his palm to his forehead. "God, I must have been messed up hard. All right, let's just place the foot under your leg and make sure it matches up."

He opened the satchel and removed the detached, glass slipper-shod foot, eyeing it with disgust. He placed it on the floor and slid it in the space under the stepsister's leg. He blinked suddenly in bewilderment. He looked at the stepsister's foot. He looked at the glass slipper-shod foot. He took a step back, scratched his head and sighed out his nose. A few seconds later, he blinked again and looked up with a frown.

"Wait a minute!" he bellowed. "You're missing your right foot! This one is a left foot!"

A look of horror crossed the stepsister's face as she realized how unbelievably stupid she'd been in having the wrong foot amputated. The stepmother grimaced. "By the way, Prince," she said. "About the ball, I was wondering what you thought of your mysterious companion's dancing?"

"I don't remember," the prince replied. "Like I said, I got wasted. What's it to you?"

She poked the older stepsister spitefully. "I always told her she had two left feet."

The prince looked at her, puzzled, and the stepsister broke down sobbing.

It was then that the younger stepsister smugly hopped into the room, sat down next to her inconsolable sister, and raised her gown to reveal her own missing left foot. She cleared her throat loudly.

The stepmother gasped and her face lit up. She wanted to gush with praise for her younger daughter, but it would obviously have to wait.

The prince gawked at the younger stepsister. "What the frig?" he asked. "You're missing a foot, too?"

"Yes!" she replied. "It was painfully severed last night as I was leaving the palace as a result of…some…unfortunate incident."

The prince shook his head and sighed as he gently placed the foot under her leg. As he did, he couldn't help noticing that her right foot was significantly larger than the one in the slipper. He frowned as he leaned back, and eyed her disdainfully.

"No way is this your foot!" he said, with narrowed eyes.

"Of course it is! I just have different-sized feet. That's not so unusual, is it?"

"Well," the prince belched. "I know for a fact you don't have a shoe to match this one."

"What makes you so sure?"

The prince leaned in angrily toward her. "Because they don't make clown shoes out of glass!"

The messenger tapped the prince on the shoulder. "It would appear, your highness, that these young women attempted to deceive you by severing one of their lower extremities."

The prince turned around and sneered at him, and clapped his hands slowly. "Way to go, Sherlock!" he said. He stepped back and glared at the stepsisters. "Man!" he said, "I can't believe you chicks had your feet chopped off just for a shot at my dong. That's insane! But, you know, that's not *just* insane. That's not *just* dishonest." He crossed his arms and looked down his nose at them. "That's just plain shallow!"

Just then, Cinderelleper entered the room, hopping frantically toward the outside door. She desperately wanted to avoid the prince, but she couldn't hide any longer, as the house had no indoor plumbing, and her bladder was precariously full.

"Hey, you!" the prince shouted suspiciously. "What are you hoppin' around for?"

Cinderelleper froze in place and silently stood on one leg as the prince slowly advanced toward her. As he made his way around the couch, he could clearly see her standing on one leg.

The prince's eyes bulged and he furiously shook his head. "What the hell?" he shouted. He looked up at the ceiling and extended his arms with his palms facing up. "Is anyone in this friggin' house <u>not</u> missing a foot?" In desperation, he turned to the messenger. "Lackey, let's get the hell out of here; these bitches are crazy!"

The messenger, needing to see for himself, rushed to the prince's side and gazed at Cinderelleper. "Just a moment, your highness," he said. "This young lady is wearing a glass slipper!"

Cinderelleper glanced down and realized she was wearing the

other glass slipper. She shut her eyes tightly, clenched her fists, and silently shouted curse words in her head.

"Hey, yeah!" The prince beamed. "And her glass slipper's a perfect match for the one with the foot in it!" he declared. "I remember now! She's the one who looks like Edwina! At last I've found my princess bride!" He embraced an unwilling Cinderelleper and kissed her ferociously.

The stepmother angrily stood up. "Now, just a minute!" she said. "How can she be the one? She wasn't at the ball last night!"

Sternly removing herself from the prince's embrace, Cinderelleper rolled her eyes. "Yes, I was there. You spoke directly to me and I told you I was a duchess. For some reason, all it took was a makeover for me to become completely unrecognizable to you."

The younger stepsister sadly sighed. "Now it makes sense," she said, "that she would be the one to lose her foot. Accidentally, I mean."

The prince scratched his head. "How does that 'make sense', you friggin' lunatic?"

The younger stepsister eyed the prince distastefully. "She lost her foot because she has leprosy."

"Oh!" said the prince, in dawning realization. "I got it now!" He looked back at Cinderelleper. "I was wondering how that hap…"

The prince went silent as a stopped gear seemed to budge from behind his eyes. He winced in unmitigated repulsion and took a shaky step backward. "Y-you…" he choked, "you're a leper?"

"I'm afraid so," she replied, casually swinging her leg.

The prince shuddered. He glanced around the room, at the

two stepsisters and down again at Cinderelleper's dismembered foot and her leg gently swaying above it. He looked up to see a macabre grin on Cinderelleper's face. "So when's the wedding, lover boy?" she asked.

The prince tightly shut his eyes, pulled at his hair and screamed. "I'm getting out of here!"

The messenger worriedly looked on as the prince bolted out the door. "Your highness!" he shouted. He politely excused himself, absentmindedly picked up the satchel and foot, and dashed out after the prince.

Four seconds later, he ran back in and handed Cinderelleper her foot. "Here," he said, awkwardly pressing it into her hands. "You can have this back. I doubt we'll be needing it again." He grimaced and shook his wrists, then turned and ran out the door again.

The stepmother sighed and sat down heavily. "I feel so defeated," she said.

The stepsisters exchanged glances. "You?" asked the older one. "How do you think *we* feel?"

The stepmother turned to them. "I don't want to hear it," she said. "You two should have known your schemes didn't have a leg to stand on."

Cinderelleper desperately hopped outside to avoid wetting herself.

The stepmother buried her face in her hands. "I can't believe it," she moaned. "We had the kingdom within our clutches and lost it, all because of Cinderelleper's leprosy. How could she do this to us?"

"The worst part of all," the younger stepsister said, "is how she went to the ball behind our backs. If she'd just been straight with us, we could have struck a deal to keep her leprosy a secret until after the wedding!"

The stepmother glared at her. "Well, you're the one who blabbed it, you dingbat!" she said.

"Yeah, but it's still Cinderelleper's fault!"

"How is it her fault?"

The stepsister shrugged. "Because it's always her fault."

The stepmother frowned wickedly. "Yes," she said. "And is she going to get it for this one!" She glanced around the room. "Where did she go?"

The older stepsister yawned and rubbed her eyes. "She's mostly outside."

"What do you mean 'mostly?'"

"There's a bit of her still in here. She left her foot on the floor."

"Well, then, let's go find the part of her that can still feel pain! Hobble this way, girls!"

***

When they located Cinderelleper in the yard, she was in the midst of a conversation with her fairy godmother.

"I'm so sorry, dear," the fairy said. "I hope I didn't embarrass you. I swear, of all the inopportune times to suddenly appear."

Cinderelleper straightened her gown. "It's fine, Godma. It's my fault for not waiting 'til I reached the outhouse. Besides, I'm just glad to see you."

"And I'm very proud to see you, my dear! You couldn't have handled the situation better. The kingdom is surely safe from your stepmother's influence, and it's all thanks to you!"

Cinderelleper sighed as she felt a foreboding tingling sensation in her elbow. "At least I can die knowing that I made a difference."

"That's right, and, Oh! I just remembered! Since I last saw you, I've figured out the cure for leprosy! It's within my power to save you after all!"

Cinderelleper gasped. "That's wonderful!" she cried.

"And, now, I'll just wave my magic wand, and—"

"There you are!" the stepmother shouted as she marched over to where Cinderelleper was standing. She fiercely grabbed her by the forearm, which came off in her hand. Taken aback, the stepmother stared for a moment at the arm, then angrily threw it on the ground and resumed her abusive agenda.

"When I'm through with you," she growled, "you'll wish there was even less of you to injure!" She looked menacingly at the fairy godmother. "And who is this fat, dippy old broad?"

The fairy godmother sneered and rolled up her sleeves. She slowly ascended from the ground, and loomed as thunderclouds formed around her. An echo could be heard across the land as she spoke. "I'm the law, honey!" she roared.

She violently waved her magic wand, pointed it at the stepmother, and transformed her into a living, sentient pile of horse manure. As disturbing as it was to witness, the horrified scream that emanated from it made it even worse.

The stepsisters shrieked. Cinderelleper gasped. The fairy descended to the ground looking shocked at her own creation.

"Jeez, Godma!" said Cinderelleper. "She obviously had a big comeuppance in store, but a pile of dung? A live pile of dung?

Don't you think that's a bit extreme?"

The fairy put her fingers to her lips. "Oh, dear," she said. "I must admit, I see your point. I suppose I could have acted with more restraint, but…she's…she's just such a bitch, you know?"

"You don't have to explain to me," Cinderelleper muttered.

The pile of horse manure churned in a manner one could interpret as malicious. "Hey!" it shouted. "Who do you think you're calling a bitch?"

The fairy blushed and covered her eyes with her hand. "Oh, my, I'm so sorry. Where are my manners?"

"What? You're sorry?" the poopy stepmother asked. "You turned me into a pile of crap and you're concerned about your manners? Change me back this instant!"

The fairy thought for a moment. "I'll consider it. But at the moment, I've got more important things to do."

She waved her wand again, and chanted, "Boogerty, Boobity, Koo Koo Ka—Choo!" magically curing Cinderelleper of her leprosy, reattaching her body parts, and making her immune to accumulating cinders so she could never legitimately be called "Cinderella," "Elleper," or any other asinine nicknames derived from the combination of her name, cinders, and leprosy ever again. In essence, she restored Ella to her former self.

With her jaw dropped, Ella gazed at her fairy godmother, tears of joy streaming from her eyes. "Oh, Godma!" she cried. "Thank you! Thank you so much!"

"A pleasure, dearie."

The younger stepsister meekly addressed the fairy. "Excuse me, ma'am."

The fairy raised her eyebrow and emitted a long, drawn out,

"Yes?"

"I…I know my sister and I were kind of mean to Cinderelleper. Wait! I mean Ella! Ella! But I think we've seen the error of our ways."

The fairy crossed her arms. "Oh, have you now?" she asked.

"Oh, yes, definitely!" The younger stepsister replied.

"Yes, completely, ma'am!" the older sister added, with a frenzied nodding of her head.

"And watching you turn our mother into a heap of turds has been a just punishment for our misdeeds, but we were wondering…"

The fairy rolled her eyes. "You two are ruining Ella's moment, but go on."

"Well, we were wondering if you could reattach our feet like you did with Cinderel— I mean Ella! Like you did with Ella. We would be most grateful."

"Most grateful," the older stepsister echoed.

The fairy glanced wearily at Ella and turned back to the sisters. "You're asking me to reattach them when you're the ones who decided to cut them off?"

"Yes, ma'am."

The fairy godmother sighed.

"Well, I'm sorry, girls, but it's beyond my power. We have a saying in Fairyland about magic, and that is, 'you can't fix stupid.' And you can't. Not with fairy magic; not even with duct tape."

Ella smirked. "Wow, Godma," she said. "Touché. But speaking of fairy magic, I don't care what anyone says, curing my leprosy and healing me makes you a miracle-worker in my book!"

Don't be silly, dear," the fairy godmother replied. "Miracles are only make-believe. You of all people should know that. Anyway, I've got to go now. Bye!"

"Wait!" the pile of horse manure screamed. "I thought you were going to consider changing me back!"

"Nah," said the fairy godmother. "I just said that to shut you up so I could get on with fixing Ella. And to give you false hope so I could devastate you a second time. You deserve it, you pile of horse crap. But look on the bright side; I also made you <u>immortal</u>! You're never, *ever* going to die. Even after I die, Ella dies, your kids die, everyone in the entire world dies, the human race goes extinct, and after the sun engulfs the Earth, the entire solar system collapses and the sun explodes, you'll still be a pile of crap and fully aware that you're a pile of crap. You'll *literally always* be a pile of crap."

The pile of crap was speechless. The stepsisters were speechless. Ella was speechless.

In the silence, the fairy fidgeted with her wand. "Well, I guess that wraps things up here," she said. "I'm going to go now, but I'll be watching over you, Ella. I'll be sure to keep you safe from now on. Just remember, your fairy godmother loves you."

One last time, the fairy godmother waved her magic wand and arose into the sky like a slowly rising firework, leaving a trail of white, sparkly light particles behind her as she vanished into the twilight sky.

Ella stared up at the sky with her mouth hanging open. "Holy cripes," she said to her stepsisters. "I am so glad I never got on her bad side."

"Oh, Ella," the younger stepsister said. "I'm so sorry for how badly I treated you. I'll never be the same."

"Same for me, Ella," said the older stepsister. "I never realized just how much our mother influenced us. And even if my sister and I weren't terrified of your fairy godmother's wrath, we'd never mistreat you again."

Ella couldn't help feeling touched. Even though she was implicitly assured of never being mistreated again thanks to her fairy godmother, she trusted that her stepsister's remorse was genuine.

"Well, I don't know about you two," Ella said, "but after hiding in the basement and not eating all day, I'm hungry. What do you say we go inside, make some dinner, and dine tonight as sisters?"

The stepsisters smiled. "That sounds great," said the younger.

As the young ladies motioned to return indoors, the pile of manure stirred. "What about me?" it asked.

The older stepsister looked behind at the mound and consulted her younger sibling. "What do you think Mother would do to us if we brought a big load of poop into the house?"

"She'd fly off the handle and probably beat us senseless," the younger replied. "I think we should just leave it outside."

"Agreed. That's the way Mother would have wanted it."

"But *I am* your mother!" the mound wailed.

The younger stepsister sneered. "You're invincible horse-potty that will outlast every star in the entire galaxy. You surely don't need shelter or food to survive."

The pile of horse-potty writhed. "But deep down inside, I'm still your mother. I still have my heart, my mind, my personality!"

The sisters exchanged glances. "Yes, mother, and those are

the parts of you we can *really* do without."

The three young women went inside and closed the door.

***

Later that evening, Ella sat on her straw mat in the basement (she hadn't yet decided which room of the house she was going to move into), enjoying the fire, relishing her new immunity to cinders, sipping a glass of wine, and sharing some gourmet cheese with Driver mouse.

"Well, my little friend," she said. "here's to a future with hope." She raised her glass and then swallowed the remaining wine with a hearty gulp. She tipsily reached for the bottle, and, pouring herself yet another glass, glanced down at Driver with a silly grin.

"Hey, Driver," she said, "you like merlot?" She poured a few drops on the floor in front of the mouse, who sniffed it and quickly lapped it up. He sat up on his hind legs and rubbed his belly with a satisfied squeak.

The squeak became a series of squeaks, and the series of squeaks seemed to take on a melodic quality. If Ella didn't know better, she would have sworn the little mouse was humming a tune.

Ella examined her bottle of wine. "I think that's enough for me," she said.

Unable to help himself, Driver's humming escalated to singing: *"If you keep on believing that dream…in your heart…"* Needless to say, he didn't quite remember the words.

Ella impulsively removed one of her glass slippers and gently hit Driver over the head with it. The mouse abruptly stopped singing, rubbed his head with a paw, and glared up at Ella with his whiskers twitching.

"Well, what did I tell you about singing?" Ella scolded. She lifted the wineglass to her lips as she stared into space. "Stupid singing mice and their creepy-ass chipmunk voices," she muttered. "What kind of sick mind comes up with stuff like that?"

THE END

Epilogue

One might ask, "What is the point of this rendition of the Cinderella story?" Our heroine doesn't end up becoming a princess. In the end, her only consolation for all her troubles is to end up *not* afflicted with leprosy, and *not* missing body parts. So her "happy ending" is that she's no longer suffering, and that the people who have contributed to her suffering are essentially incapable of harming her further.

Perhaps that's all the happy ending she would have wanted. Oh, and she got a pair of highly fashionable glass slippers out of the deal, too, so that's pretty cool.

As far as her stepsisters are concerned, though they were antagonists undeserving of sympathy, their circumstances at the story's end suggest they may end up as better people as a result of learning from their self-imposed misfortunes. Whether they do or not isn't really important, because they're just the stepsisters, and nobody really cares about them.

But what of the wicked stepmother? Are we to feel sympathy for her? Does the fairy godmother not appear a bit wicked herself for imposing such an impossibly cruel fate? Was the wicked stepmother actually deserving of being granted immortality as a pile of feces? Could anyone deserve that?

As it turns out, the stepmother suffered deeply for many long years. The humiliation and hopelessness of her situation was a source of unimaginable torment. But it couldn't last indefinitely. At some point, she realized that accepting her fate was the only rational choice she could possibly make. She could either accept it, or continue in rejecting the truth of her situation and continue to suffer for an untold number of years, if not lifetimes.

Over time, her attitude changed to one of serenity. Hundreds of years after her initial transformation, the immortal pile of dookie not only found a godlike peace within herself, but people began to regard her as something of a sage. Having found a perfect inner peace despite her condition, she could comfort anyone. Word spread of the wisdom of the talking pile of poop, and in time she became the closest thing to a god that the people of a certain time could ever hope to know.

All of the ancient religions came to be seen as simply myths of a more primitive time. Humanity, as a whole, could not deny the existence of the all-knowing, ever-living pile of horse-doodie. By the sheer duration of her existence, and the wisdom and understanding she cultivated in the inconceivable span of her life, she eventually united the entire planet in world peace.

Of course, the human race could only last so long, and when it died out, the poopy stepmother had to spend many more years alone in deep contemplation. In due time, the Earth itself ceased to be, and the stepmotherly pile of crap was set adrift aimlessly in space.

Several thousand more years later, some members of an alien race, known as "Zyrplexians" came along in a spaceship and discovered her. They took her to their home planet, where the people grew to revere and worship her. In the span of a few generations, she came to be known as the alien culture's most prominent figure, an uncontested designation for as long as life on planet Zyrplex endured. Statues were painstakingly rendered in her honor, and the people commonly wore necklaces with jewel pendants made in her sacred, poopy image.

In the end, the evil stepmother who tormented Cinderella, and who was turned into a living, talking pile of horse manure, lived on to become the greatest sentient being in the history of the entire universe.

This brings us to the final question of what became of the situation at the royal palace. Did the prince end up finding a woman to become the princess and the mother of his children?

Nope.

As it turns out, not two weeks after the grand ball, the royal messenger, apparently at his wit's end, and in a fit of blind rage, attacked and brutally killed the prince. But he made it look like an accident, got away with it, and lived out the rest of his days with a clear conscience and an inward smile.

And you thought fairy tales were simple.

Also by Ford Forkum:

Alien Invasion of the Zombie Apocalypse

In a satirical combination of two end-of-the-world scenarios, a zombie plague is quickly followed by an alien invasion in a time when humanity is already struggling with vampires.

Landing dead center at a college campus swarming with zombies, the aliens soon realize that their abduction mission is going to be quite a bit more complicated than they'd imagined. The presence of vampires only makes the situation worse.

Will the human race prevail or be forced to relocate to an alien planet? Is there any way to reverse the zombie plague? Is the plague contagious to aliens and can an alien be turned into a vampire? What if a vampire alien became a zombie, then was bitten by a radioactive spider and then possessed by the ghost of a robot werewolf? That last part doesn't happen in the story, but what if it did?

Find out what becomes of humanity in this hodgepodge of dystopian absurdity.

★★★★★ "Jokes left and right. Very entertaining. Highly recommended!"
- *Oleg Medvedkov*

★★★★★ "The tone of this book reminds me a great deal of the works of Terry Pratchett and Douglas Adams. Recommended if you like to laugh (and who doesn't?)"
- *K. Sozaeva*

★ "This story was horrible. I felt like I was reading something written by a 9 year old."
– *Name Withheld*

Available at Amazon in the US:
http://www.amazon.com/dp/B00806SB5W
And in the UK: http://www.amazon.co.uk/dp/B00806SB5W

Beers In Heaven (A Modern Afterlife Novel)

Heaven...what is this "Heaven," anyway? Well, you won't find it on a celestial map, and the only way to get there is to die!

Whether you're a fundamentalist Christian who's morally superior to everyone, or a condescending atheist who knows everything, you're in for a big surprise: Supernatural power in the hands of immortal humans guarantees anything but a tranquil prolonged existence, especially since exile to Hell for too many screw-ups remains a possible threat.

Enter the spirit of college dropout Zack Preston. After being scanned by Heavensoft Judge (the Automated Spirit Judgment Software), he floats onward to Heaven. Becoming aware of his postmortem condition, he tries to put the pieces of his brief past life together with the help of Stan Vidale, his orientation guide.

Through Zack's surreal and absurd tribulations in adjusting to modern afterlife culture, you'll see how Heaven works to accommodate its ever-increasing population of dead people who have nothing but time on their hands.

Surreal satire and irreverence awaits all who seek a new meaning of "divine comedy."

★★★★★ "Love, love, love, love this novel and Forkum's wacky sense of humor. I cannot give this funny and clever novel

anything less than five stars and eagerly await the next work by this fabulous author."
- *Rabid Readers Reviews*

★★★★ "Memorable: I initially expected to find Beers in Heaven humorous, and I did."
- *Jaks R*

★★★★★ "I thought this would be straight comedy, some satire, but not as thought provoking as it turned out to be."
- *Wendy's Mom*

Available at Amazon in the US:
https://www.amazon.com/dp/B00FI8I8I0
And in the UK: https://www.amazon.co.uk/dp/B00FI8I8I0

About the Author

Ford Forkum is a writer and media maker from The Great Northeast. His unbridled imagination and humor resonate with readers who have a taste for subtle sarcasm, mockery of popular culture, and absurdity that ventures to the hazy outskirts of reality.

His first book, the comedic science fiction short story, Alien Invasion of the Zombie Apocalypse made Amazon.com's top ten bestseller list in the satire category, and was nominated for the eFestival of Words Independent Author Awards in the science fiction category.

Visit Ford's homepage at www.fordforkum.com.